Disney's Two-Minute Classics

Adapted by MARY PACKARD

A GOLDEN BOOK • NEW YORK

Western Publishing Company, Inc., Racine, Wisconsin 53404

ISBN: 0-307-12180-1/ISBN: 0-307-62180-4 (lib. bdg.)   F G H I J K L M

Cinderella

Once upon a time, in a faraway land, there lived a sweet and pretty girl named Cinderella. She lived with her mean old stepmother and two mean and ugly stepsisters. They made Cinderella work day and night, cooking, cleaning, and taking care of them.

One day an invitation came from the palace of the king. A great ball was being given for the prince, and every girl in the kingdom was invited.

"How lovely!" said Cinderella. "I am invited, too."

"You!" shrieked her stepsisters. "The prince's ball for you?" They kept Cinderella busy all week long getting them ready for the ball.

A coach pulled up to the door on the evening of the ball. "Why, Cinderella!" said the cruel stepsisters. "You're not ready for the ball!"

"No," said Cinderella sadly. "I guess I can't go."

Cinderella ran into the garden and began to weep. Suddenly a little old woman appeared. She was Cinderella's fairy godmother!

"Hurry, child!" she said. "You're going to the ball!"

Then, with a wave of her hand, the fairy godmother turned a fat pumpkin into a splendid coach. Cinderella's pet mice became horses and her dog a fine footman. Best of all, Cinderella's ragged dress was transformed into the loveliest ball gown that ever was. On her feet were two tiny glass slippers.

"Oh, how can I ever thank you?" said Cinderella.

"Just have a wonderful time, dear," said the fairy godmother. "And be sure to be home before twelve. The magic only lasts until midnight."

At the king's palace every lady in the land was dressed beautifully. But Cinderella was the loveliest of them all. The prince never left her side.

Suddenly the clock began to strike midnight. Without a word, Cinderella ran out of the ballroom and down the palace stairs. She lost one glass slipper on her way. The prince tried to find her, but no one knew where she had gone.

The next morning the grand duke went from house to house with the glass slipper. The prince had said he would marry no one but the girl who had worn the tiny shoe.

Every girl in the land tried to put it on. The ugly stepsisters tried hardest of all. But no one could wear the tiny shoe.

Cinderella was locked in her room. Her stepsisters were taking no chances. But luckily her little friends the mice got her stepmother's key. They pushed it under Cinderella's door just in time.

As the grand duke was about to leave Cinderella's house, she called out, "Please let me try the slipper on!"

Of course, the slipper fitted perfectly, since it was her very own. At last the long search was over.

And so Cinderella became the prince's bride, and they lived happily ever after.

Pinocchio

Kind old Geppetto stood at his workbench and carved a puppet that looked just like a real boy. Jiminy Cricket chirped merrily.

"There," said Geppetto. "You're finished. I think I'll call you Pinocchio."

Geppetto looked at the clock. "Well," he said, "it's time for bed." He placed Pinocchio on the workbench. Then he opened the window, and the light of the evening star streamed into the room.

"Star light, star bright . . ." he said softly, "I wish Pinocchio were a real live boy!" Then he climbed into bed and fell fast asleep.

Jiminy Cricket was still awake when suddenly the cottage was filled with light.

The Blue Fairy flew to the workbench where little wooden Pinocchio sat and said, "Awake, Pinocchio, and live. Be good and brave, and someday you will grow to be a real live boy."

The Blue Fairy asked Jiminy to be Pinocchio's conscience, to tell him the difference between right and wrong. "Be a good boy, Pinocchio," the Blue Fairy said, "and always let your conscience be your guide."

The next morning Geppetto was delighted to discover Pinocchio running around. "It's a miracle!" Geppetto said.

Then Pinocchio started off for his first day of school. But he never made it. Instead, he ran off with the sly old fox J. Worthington Foulfellow and his partner, Gideon, the bad cat.

"Pinoke," Jiminy Cricket called, "don't do it!"

But although the Blue Fairy had told Pinocchio always to listen to Jiminy Cricket's advice, Pinocchio ignored his little friend.

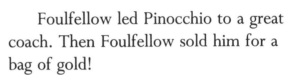

Foulfellow led Pinocchio to a great coach. Then Foulfellow sold him for a bag of gold!

The coach was pulled by six sad donkeys. It was filled with boys of all sizes. Pinocchio made friends with the leader, a loud bully named Lampwick. The coach was going to a place called Pleasure Island.

Pleasure Island was wonderful. Every day the boys played. They ate candy and ice cream and cake. They broke windows and had mud fights. What fun Pinocchio was having!

Then Pinocchio noticed something strange was happening. Little by little, Lampwick's ears grew long and fuzzy. Then he grew a tail. Soon Lampwick was no longer a boy. He was a donkey!

Pinocchio felt his own head. He had two donkey ears. Then Pinocchio looked down and discovered that he had a tail, too!

"Aha!" cried the coachman. "Two more donkeys to sell to the salt mines!"

He put a rope around Lampwick's neck and was about to do the same to Pinocchio when Jiminy cried, "Run, Pinocchio, run!"

Pinocchio and Jiminy Cricket ran to the edge of the island, dived into the water, and swam away.

When they got home, Geppetto was not there. He left a note saying that he was out looking for Pinocchio.

Jiminy and Pinocchio set out to find Geppetto. It was a long and dangerous journey, but Pinocchio was determined to find his father. He finally found Geppetto inside a fierce whale and bravely helped Geppetto home.

The Blue Fairy had been watching over Pinocchio the whole time. "You have learned your lesson well, Pinocchio," she said. "You have been brave and good." And as her magic wand touched him, Pinocchio felt himself turn into a real boy!

Geppetto hugged his son and laughed with joy. And as for Jiminy Cricket, the fairy gave him a badge of gold. It said:

Awarded
to a Good Conscience
who helped make
a Real Boy out of a
Wooden Head.

Dumbo

Dumbo, Mrs. Jumbo's baby boy, was the littlest elephant in the circus and had two of the biggest, floppiest ears. Everyone but Mrs. Jumbo thought his ears were just plain ridiculous. When the audience laughed at Dumbo, the other elephants were ashamed.

One day a bunch of bullies came to the circus. They teased Dumbo, and then they began to pinch and poke him. Dumbo's mother ran to the rescue and gave those bullies the spankings they deserved.

The bullies cried, "Help! Help! Wild elephant on the run!" Everyone panicked and raced for the exits. Circus guards locked Mrs. Jumbo in a cage.

The other elephants blamed Dumbo for giving them a bad name. But the ringmaster had plans for Dumbo. He tried Dumbo in several different roles, but the little elephant's ears always got in the way. At last he decided to make Dumbo a clown. Dumbo had to dress like a baby and jump out of a fake burning building.

The act was a huge success, but Dumbo was very scared and very sad.

One night Dumbo's friend, Timothy Mouse, took Dumbo for a walk in the countryside. Far into the night they frolicked in the moonlight.

Soon it was morning. Timothy was surprised to find that he and Dumbo were perched in the top branch of a tall tree, with a flock of crows for company.

"How did we get up here?" asked Timothy.

"You must have flown," said a crow. "It's easy," he added. "Just flap your wings." The crow pointed to Dumbo's big ears. "Here," said the crow, handing Dumbo a shiny black feather. "Hold on to this and you can't help but fly."

Dumbo flapped his ears. He swooped and soared. What fun it was to fly!

Dumbo and Timothy got back to the circus just in time for the show. Once more Dumbo found himself atop a burning building. This time, instead of dropping down into the net, Dumbo glided gracefully through the air.

But when the magic feather slipped from his trunk, he began to plummet. Dumbo would have crashed if he hadn't heard Timothy say, "Come on, Dumbo. You don't need that feather. You can do it!"

Dumbo gave a mighty flap, and soon he was flying higher than ever.

From that day on, Dumbo was a star. And Mrs. Jumbo was famous, too, for she was the mother of the only flying elephant in the world!

Lady and the Tramp

Lady was a cocker spaniel who came to live with two people called Darling and Jim Dear. Lady had two feeding bowls of her own. She had a basket with a blanket in it. She trained her people to feed her from the table—just a bit now and then. And she trained them to let her sleep at the foot of their beds. Lady was very happy living there.

One day Lady met a dog named Tramp. "I'll wear no man's collar!" Tramp boasted proudly.

"But where do you sleep?" Lady asked him. "And what do you do for food?"

"Ah, that's easy if you know your way around," said Tramp. "And you'll see, things will be different someday when a baby comes to your house to stay. For there's only so much room for love in people's hearts."

Lady remembered Tramp's words when a baby did come to her house to live.

Darling and Jim Dear had no time for her now. They were too busy with the baby. And worst of all, Darling's Aunt Sarah came.

"That dog!" Aunt Sarah said. "She must stay out in the yard, and she'll have to wear a muzzle!"

"Oh, no!" said Tramp when he saw Lady. "So it's happened already! Well, we'll get rid of that muzzle before you know it."

Tramp led Lady straight to the zoo, where they met the Beaver. He was glad to chew off Lady's muzzle.

Lady turned to Tramp and said, "I must go home now. I have to watch the house and the baby."

When Lady returned home, Aunt Sarah chained her to a post in the yard. Lady was keeping an eye on the house when she saw a mean and ugly rat climbing in the window to the baby's room.

Tramp heard Lady's barks and came running to help. Lady snapped her leash, and the two dogs raced inside the house. Tramp caught the rat, who had been ready to pounce on the baby.

Jim Dear and Darling appeared in the doorway of the room. "Good girl!" Jim said, patting Lady on the head. "And many thanks to you, too, fellow," he said to Tramp. "It looks as if you've found yourself a home."

Now Lady and Tramp have two families to look after. Darling and Jim Dear and the baby are one. And the other is a fine family of four pups of their very own!

Peter Pan

Once upon a time there were three children—Wendy, John, and Michael Darling. They liked bedtime, because every night in their nursery Wendy told them stories about Peter Pan.

Peter was a boy who decided he would never grow up. He lived in a faraway place called Never Land. Sometimes Peter himself, and Tinker Bell the pixie, would come flying down and sit on the nursery windowsill to hear the stories.

One night Peter asked the children to come to Never Land with him. The children were delighted. Peter taught them how to fly. All it took was a wish and a pinch of pixie dust, and they were off!

Never Land was a wonderful and magical place. There were fairies living in the treetops, and mermaids swimming in a lagoon. There were real Indians living in a village on a cliff, and woods full of wild animals.

Wendy, John, and Michael loved Never Land. They liked Peter's underground house and the Lost Boys who lived there. And the Lost Boys loved to hear Wendy's bedtime stories.

But there was also danger in Never Land. There was a ship full of pirates who sailed the seas, looking for trouble. The leader was a wicked man named Captain Hook. Once, in a fair fight, Peter Pan had cut off one of the captain's hands, and now he wore a hook instead.

"I'll catch that Peter Pan if it's the last thing I do!" vowed Captain Hook. He kidnapped Wendy, Peter, Michael, and the Lost Boys.

"Don't worry," said Wendy to the boys. "Peter will save us!"

Wendy was right. Just as Captain Hook was ordering Wendy to walk the plank, Peter appeared. He beat Captain Hook in a sword fight. Then he freed all of his friends. Peter and the boys scared the pirates into jumping overboard.

"Hurray!" cried Peter. "The pirates are gone! Where shall we sail the ship?"

"I'm afraid it's time for us to go home now," said Wendy. And with a wish and a pinch of pixie dust, they made the pirate ship fly, all the way back to the nursery window.

The three children were glad to be home again, but they knew they would never forget their adventures with Peter Pan.

Bambi

One spring morning in the forest a little fawn was born. All the birds and animals came to see him, for he was a very special fawn.

"What will you name the young prince?" asked Thumper the rabbit.

"I will call him Bambi," said the fawn's mother.

The forest was filled with friends. Thumper and the other animals played with Bambi nearly every day. Faline, another fawn, played with them, too.

The seasons passed, and one morning when Bambi awoke, everything was covered with white.

Bambi saw Thumper sliding on the frozen pond. "Come on!" said Thumper. "The water's stiff!"

But when Bambi trotted out on the ice, his front legs shot forward and he crashed!

"That's okay," said Thumper, laughing. "We can play something else!"

The months passed. Bambi and his mother were nibbling some bark from a tree, when all of a sudden they heard loud hoofbeats. A herd of stags came galloping toward them. They were led by the great prince of the forest. He said just one word, "Man." All the birds and animals followed him back into the woods. They heard frightening roaring noises behind them as they ran.

"Run for the thicket!" cried Bambi's mother.

When Bambi reached safety, his mother was nowhere in sight. The prince of the forest appeared beside him.

"Your mother can't be with you anymore," the prince said. "You must learn to walk alone."

At last spring arrived in the forest. Bambi was growing into a handsome buck. One day he met a graceful doe in the woods. "Who are you?" he asked.

"Don't you remember me?" she said. "I'm Faline."

Bambi and Faline spent that spring and summer together, frolicking through the woods and meadows.

One morning Bambi sniffed the scent of man again. He smelled something else, too—smoke! Once again the prince appeared.

"The forest has caught fire from the flames of man's campfires," said the prince. "We must go to the river. But first we must warn the other animals."

When they were all safely at the river's edge, the prince said, "When the forest is green again, I will be very old. Bambi, you must take my place then." Bambi bowed his head.

When spring came, green leaves and grass covered the scars left by the fire. All the woodland animals came to call on Faline and her two spotted fawns.

Not far away was Bambi, the proud father and the new prince of the forest.

Snow White

Once upon a time a lovely daughter was born to a king and queen. She had lips as red as blood, skin as white as snow, and hair as black as ebony. They called her Snow White.

After Snow White was born, her mother died. Many years later, Snow White's father married again.

His new wife was beautiful, but her heart was cold and cruel. She was vain, too. The queen's most prized possession was a magic mirror. Every day she asked the mirror, "Mirror, mirror, on the wall, who is the fairest of us all?"

As long as the mirror answered with the queen's name, she was happy. But Snow White was growing up to be more and more beautiful, and the queen was jealous.

The day the queen had been dreading finally arrived.

"Mirror, mirror, on the wall, who is the fairest of us all?" she asked.

"She is Snow White," answered the mirror.

The queen flew into a rage. "Take Snow White into the forest and bring me back her heart in this jeweled box," she ordered her huntsman.

But the huntsman could not kill the sweet girl. "Run into the forest and hide," he warned Snow White. "Never return to the castle."

Alone in the forest, Snow White wept with fright, but she was not really alone. All the little woodland animals were her friends, and chirping and chattering, they led her to a new home.

Inside the cottage, the sink was piled with unwashed dishes and everything was covered with dust.

"Maybe the children who live here need someone to keep house for them," said Snow White. With the help of her woodland friends, Snow White soon had the little house spic and span.

The seven little men, known as the Seven Dwarfs, came home from work. They knew at once that something had changed. They crept upstairs, where they found Snow White just waking up from a nap.

"Oh!" cried Snow White. "I know who you are." She had read their names on their beds. "You're Dopey and Sneezy and Happy and Grumpy and Doc and Bashful and Sleepy!"

Snow White told the Seven Dwarfs about the wicked queen's plot. "You must stay and live with us!" said the Dwarfs.

Meanwhile, the queen found out from the mirror that Snow White was still alive. Disguised as an old woman, the queen found her way to the little cottage in the forest. In her hand was a poisoned apple.

The queen knocked at the door. Snow White could not resist the juicy red apple. She took a bite and sank lifeless to the floor.

The grieving Dwarfs laid Snow White on a bed of gold and crystal. They kept watch over her day and night.

One day a handsome prince came to the forest to see Snow White. Charmed with her beauty, he kissed her. At last Snow White awoke! The Seven Dwarfs danced with joy, and the prince carried Snow White off to his castle in the clouds.

Sleeping Beauty

Once upon a time a daughter was born to a king and queen of a faraway land. They named the child Aurora. To honor the baby princess, the king held a great feast. Among the guests were three good fairies. Each of them wished to bless the infant with a gift.

"My gift shall be the gift of beauty," said the first fairy.

"Mine shall be the gift of song," said the second fairy.

But before the third fairy could name her gift, the castle doors flew open. The evil witch Maleficent appeared. She was angry because she hadn't been invited to the feast.

"I, too, have a gift for the newborn babe," Maleficent sneered. "Before the sun sets on her sixteenth birthday, she will prick her finger on the spindle of a spinning wheel and die!"

But the third fairy still had a gift to give, so she tried to undo the curse as best she could. She said,

"From this curse you shall wake
  When true love's kiss the spell shall break."

The king feared the witch's curse, so he allowed the good fairies to take Aurora deep into the woods to live with them. To guard their secret, they changed the baby's name to Briar Rose.

The years passed quietly, and Briar Rose grew into a beautiful young woman.

At last she reached her sixteenth birthday. Planning a surprise, the fairies sent her out to pick berries.

A handsome young man came riding by. When he heard Briar Rose singing, he jumped from his horse. Briar Rose and the young man gazed into each other's eyes. It was love at first sight.

Back at the cottage, the fairies gave Briar Rose her birthday surprise. Then Briar Rose told them that she had fallen in love.

"Impossible!" the fairies cried. They told her the truth at last—that she was a royal princess, betrothed at birth to a prince. Now it was time for her to return home.

When Maleficent learned that Aurora was home, she used her evil powers to lure her to a high tower. In the tiny room a spindle suddenly appeared.

"Touch it!" Maleficent hissed. "Touch it, I say!"

Aurora touched the spindle and instantly fell into a deep sleep.

There was only one thing to do. The good fairies found the young prince who was betrothed to Aurora, and they gave him a magic sword. With it he cut down all the thorny hedges Maleficent had put around the palace. Then he raced to the tower where Aurora lay sleeping. He kissed her. Aurora's eyes opened slowly. She was awake!

Aurora was overjoyed to learn that the young man she had met in the forest was really the prince she had been promised to at birth. They were married and lived happily ever after.